THE BOOK OF ELSIE

THE BOOK OF ELSIE

JOANNE LEVY

ORCA BOOK PUBLISHERS

Published in Canada and the United States in 2022 by Orca Book Publishers.
orcabook.com

Library and Archives Canada Cataloguing in Publication
Title: The book of Elsie / Joanne Levy.
Names: Levy, Joanne, author.
Series: Orca currents.
Description: Series statement: Orca currents
Identifiers: Canadiana (print) 20210346671 | Canadiana (ebook) 2021034668x |
ISBN 9781459834248 (softcover) | ISBN 9781459834255 (PDF) |
ISBN 9781459834262 (EPUB)
Classification: LCC PS8623.E9592 B66 2022 | DDC jC813/.6—dc23

Library of Congress Control Number: 2021948625

Summary: In this high-interest accessible novel for middle-grade readers,
Elsie comes up with a plan to save her local synagogue.

Orca Book Publishers is committed to reducing the consumption of
nonrenewable resources in the production of our books. We make
every effort to use materials that support a sustainable future.

Orca Book Publishers gratefully acknowledges the support for its publishing
programs provided by the following agencies: the Government of Canada,
the Canada Council for the Arts and the Province of British Columbia
through the BC Arts Council and the Book Publishing Tax Credit.

Edited by Tanya Trafford
Design by Ella Collier
Cover artwork by Stocksy.com/Léa Jones
Author photo by Tania Garshowitz

Printed and bound in Canada.

25 24 23 22 • 1 2 3 4

For Tanya, fierce and smart.

Chapter One

"I am going to be so fierce!"

I was so happy that I spun around and around. My hand was high in the air, holding the pretty scarf I'd just found on the twenty-five-cent rack.

Score!

It was a Saturday afternoon and I was with my best friend, Grace. We were shopping at our favorite thrift store. We came here almost every

Saturday afternoon. We loved searching for new stuff every week. You never knew what kind of treasures you'd find.

But even if we didn't find anything good, Grace and I always had fun. We loved picking through the racks of old clothes.

I was always on the lookout for cool things, but now I was on the hunt for my Queen Esther costume. I'd wear it to the Purim party at my synagogue, Temple Beth El, next month.

Abba was working on my dress. I hadn't seen it yet, but I knew it would be awesome. He was a costume designer at a theater, so he knew all about costumes.

I couldn't wait to see it. He'd tried keeping it a surprise, but I'd bugged him so much he'd finally brought home a swatch of the fabric. So now I knew it would be made of a rich green velvet. But nothing else. He was planning a big reveal.

I had the mask I'd made last year and had found the perfect sandals the month before. Now all I needed was a scarf and a crown.

And I had just found the perfect scarf. For only a quarter! It was green with gold fringes and would match the dress. Everything was coming together.

"This is the last piece I needed for my costume," I said to Grace. "Other than the crown. But I won't get one of those here."

"That would be an epic find if you did!" Grace said. "Can you imagine? Like, if some royal donated their crown by accident or something? Or it fell into their donation bag?" Grace was always thinking up stories.

"That would be awesome." I twirled again, loving how the filmy scarf floated behind me. "I guess I'd have to return it. But *after* the party."

Grace nodded. "Obviously."

"Anyway, I can get a pretend crown at the dollar store. As long as I'm fierce like the queen. That's what matters."

Grace laughed. "And beautiful. You said Queen Esther was fierce *and* beautiful."

I stopped twirling before I got dizzy. I draped the scarf around my neck and gave my bestie a bright smile. "Obviously. Queen Esther was fierce and beautiful. That's how she saved the Jews and became a superhero."

Grace rolled her eyes. "Elsie, they didn't have superheroes in those days."

"She was as close to a superhero as you get. If they made a movie about the Purim story, Gal Gadot would play her."

Grace nodded. "She's totally fierce."

It was no secret that Grace and I loved Gal Gadot as Wonder Woman. We'd each watched all the movies she was in a million times. It also wasn't a secret that I wanted to be Gal Gadot. Or that

Grace had a crush on Gal Gadot. Who could blame her?

"Anyway…" I started looking through the racks for more treasures. "I can't wait for the party."

"You've been planning for it forever," Grace said.

"Since last year's," I said. "Purim parties at the temple are so epic. Last year Rabbi Alisha gave out a prize for whoever made the most noise when they said evil Haman's name. And there's lots of yummy food. Of course, there's also the costume contest."

"Which you will win."

I nodded. I was determined to win this year.

"Purim sounds like so much fun." Grace pouted a little.

"It is," I said. "But you get Easter with all the chocolate and everything. Plus Christmas."

"Well, you get Hanukkah with doughnuts and latkes."

"That's true." I pulled a mint-green shirt off the rack and held it up against my chest.

Grace made a face. "That color is no good for you," she said. "You're too pale. It would look great against my dark skin. But you need darker colors." Grace always knew so much about colors and fashion.

I held the shirt out toward her. "Want it?"

"No thanks." She shook her head. "Not my style. I'm just saying the *color* would work on me."

I put the shirt back.

"I wish we could do some of those fun things *together*," she said. She pulled a hoodie off the rack and held it up to herself. When I shook my head, she returned it. "I like to dress up."

"We get to dress up together for Halloween," I said.

Grace sighed. "Halloween is months away. I wish I could go to your Purim party. I'd probably be the only Black Wonder Woman there."

"Probably." I put my arm around her and gave her a side hug. "And I wish you could go too. But it's only for temple members."

"I know." Grace sounded so sad.

Suddenly I got an idea. Rabbi Alisha was always talking about community outreach. She said that learning about non-Jewish people *and* teaching them about *our* customs was a good way to build a community where everyone was loved and respected.

Maybe letting my best friend come to our Purim party was a sort of outreach.

Hmm. I'd ask Rabbi Alisha at Sunday school. But I didn't want to get Grace's hopes up, just in case. So I kept my idea to myself.

I paid for my scarf and then we walked three blocks to the dollar store.

When we got inside, we went past the Easter section. Even though it was still only February and Easter was in April, the store had all the stuff out already. There was a whole row of yellow, pink and green. Baskets, colored fake grass, plastic eggs and everything bunny and baby chicken. I didn't know a lot about Easter, but it was a really colorful holiday. That was nice. Chocolate was involved, which made it even nicer.

We went through the store to the party section at the back. It bummed me out that there wasn't a specific section for Jewish holidays, but I was used to it. Our friend Sana, who is Muslim, said there wasn't a section for her people either.

In among the cheap toys there were plastic crowns hanging on pegs. I sighed. They weren't fierce. Or real. Definitely not the kind of thing the winner of the Purim costume contest would wear.

Grace pulled one off the peg and frowned at it. "It's funny that an ugly plastic crown is more expensive than that fancy scarf you got at the thrift shop."

"I know," I said. "And it's not even nice. Maybe I can make something better."

"I bet you can," she said. "You're crafty."

"Come on," I said. "Let's go."

"We can get some chocolate Easter eggs to eat on the way home."

I gave her another side hug. "You always have the best ideas."

She grinned at me. "When it includes chocolate I do. What do people eat at Purim?"

"My favorite are these special cookies called hamantaschen."

Grace stared at me. "Haman—what?"

I slowed down the word and sounded it out for her. "Ha-man-tasch-en. It's Hebrew, I think. They're shaped like triangles and have different jam fillings. My bubby makes really good ones."

"Oh, your grandmother is a great cook," Grace said. "Maybe someday I can try them." She sounded hopeful.

I couldn't wait to get to Sunday school to ask Rabbi Alisha if Grace could come to the party. The more I thought about it, the more excited I got.

I couldn't have known then that everything was about to fall apart.

Chapter Two

"What do you mean the party is canceled!"

"Elsie," Dad said, giving me a stern look. "Please stop yelling."

Seriously? He and Abba—what I called my other dad—had just told me the one thing I'd been looking forward to for an entire year had been canceled.

Abba turned back toward the fridge to finish making dinner. Like it was no big deal. It made me mad that he didn't seem to care.

Dad was setting the table but stopped to look at me. "We know you're disappointed," he said. "We are too. Abba and I were looking forward to the party as much as you were."

I doubted it.

Dad went on. "Truth is, the temple can't afford it. It's been a hard few years. It was closed during COVID. Memberships are down. People don't have much extra money to donate. There isn't enough for things like parties. In fact—"

He stopped talking when Abba made a noise and shot him a glare.

"In fact, what?" I asked. Whatever it was, it didn't sound good.

Abba sighed. He leaned back against the counter and folded his arms. He nodded at Dad.

"You may as well tell her. It won't be a secret for long."

"Secret?" I asked. Now I *had* to know.

Dad looked at me sadly. "Well," he said. "You know I'm on the board at the temple."

I nodded. Dad was the synagogue's money guy—which made sense because he was an accountant.

"We've been trying for a long time to raise funds. The building needs a lot of repairs. There are also staff salaries, equipment, books. The temple is running out of money. If we don't figure something out soon, it may have to close altogether."

What? Synagogues can't close.

Can they?

"What does that mean?"

Dad shrugged. "Just what it sounds like. We may have to sell the building. We'd have to rent space somewhere for services."

I glanced at Abba. He looked heartbroken.

"What's wrong?" I asked.

"I know it's just a building." Abba gave me a half smile. "But it's where my parents—your grandparents—got married. It's where I had my bar mitzvah. Where we had your baby-naming when we brought you home. And where we had planned…" He sniffed and shook his head.

I finished his sentence. "Where we planned to have *my* bat mitzvah too."

Abba nodded. He didn't say anything as he reached for a tissue from the box on the counter.

"What now?" I asked Dad.

"If we can't find money quickly, it's plan B," Dad said with a sigh. "There are a few options. We could maybe rent Abba's theater for some events. Ed, the manager of the funeral chapel, is on the synagogue board. He said we could do Saturday-morning services there. They don't have funerals on Shabbat so it would be available."

"What?" I said. "You can't have services at a funeral home!"

"It's just a place for people to gather, Elsie," Abba said. But then he shivered and frowned at Dad. "But I don't love the idea either."

Dad sighed. "We'll figure something out. But I'm sorry to say we won't be able to have the Purim party. There just isn't the money to finance something like that. I am sorry, Elsie. I know you've been looking forward to it."

"But I already have most of my costume!"

"There's more to the holiday than just the costume party," Abba said. "You can wear your outfit when you go to give out the Purim baskets. I'm sure everyone will love seeing you dressed up as Queen Esther."

I huffed. We'd planned to take baskets of goodies to the seniors' apartment building where my grandparents lived, but it wasn't the same.

That wasn't a party. There wouldn't be any dancing or prizes. No one would care.

I didn't want to wear my epic costume just to give out baskets to old people.

"And we can still celebrate," Dad said. "We will have a party here."

In our apartment? I looked around. It was barely big enough for the three of us to play charades on Shabbat. Dad was just trying to be nice. I knew better. There was not going to be a party.

Purim was canceled.

"Anyway," Abba said, "we'll figure that out later. Go wash up for dinner."

I turned and left the kitchen. On the way to the bathroom, I stopped in my room. I pulled the beautiful scarf out of the shopping bag. I wrapped it around my head and neck like Queen Esther would have done in olden times.

I looked in the mirror. "What would Queen Esther do?" I asked my reflection. "She would make the party happen somehow. She'd probably even save the temple while she was at it!"

Wait a minute. I had just gotten the best idea.

I was going to save the party like Queen Esther would have. And the synagogue. I was going to save everything.

Chapter Three

The next morning Abba dropped me off at the temple for Sunday school.

The building was the same as it always was. Yellow bricks, pretty stained-glass windows and giant wood doors.

But now that I knew about all the problems, it looked different. I noticed shingles missing from the roof. The ramp leading to the front doors was crumbling. The paint on the trim was peeling off.

Inside was no better. The carpet was worn, the walls were scuffed, and there were some brown water spots on the ceiling.

I'd never noticed before that the building needed so much fixing.

It made me sad.

I thought of all the parties and bar and bat mitzvahs I'd attended here. The really long services at the high holidays weren't my favorite, but I did like to sing along. Even if I didn't know the words, I'd hum and enjoy the music.

I liked to dress up for Saturday services and see my Sunday school friends. Being at temple was a part of my life as much as school was. Almost as much as home.

It was kind of like a second home.

Tears formed in my eyes. I got why Abba had been so upset. I didn't want the temple to have to close either.

I was even more determined by the time I got into our classroom. I was early for class. Mark Cohen was the only student there so far. He sat in his chair, earbuds in. His head rocked to the beat of the loud music he was listening to.

Rabbi Alisha was sitting at her desk, reading a book.

"I want to be Queen Esther!" I blurted out.

The rabbi startled and pressed her hand over her heart. "Elsie! What?"

"Sorry! I didn't mean to scare you." I walked toward her. "I meant that I want to be fierce and smart like Queen Esther."

"You *are* fierce and smart." She laughed. "But I get the feeling you have something specific in mind."

"I know about the troubles the temple is having, and I want to save it."

The smile was suddenly gone from the rabbi's face. "What do you mean?"

"My parents told me everything."

"Oh." She sighed. "I was going to tell everyone the bad news about the party today. I'm sorry, Elsie. I know you were really looking forward to it."

"No, you don't understand." I bounced on my feet, having trouble keeping my excitement inside. "I want to save the party. And the temple!"

"That would be great." Rabbi Alisha tilted her head. "But how?"

"What if we sold tickets to the party? Then we'd still get to have the party and the temple would get money. And if we made it open to anyone who wanted to come, we could sell even more tickets."

The rabbi blinked. I could tell she was thinking about my idea.

"It would be community outreach," I said, in case she wasn't convinced yet.

Her eyes lit up. "Elsie," she said with a big smile. "That is a brilliant idea. I love it!"

Of course she did. She was all about community outreach.

"We don't have a lot of time to pull it together, though," she added.

"I know," I said. "About a month. But we can do it. I will do whatever it takes to make it happen."

The rabbi grinned at me. "I know you will. Thank goodness we hadn't canceled the catering yet," she said. "Maybe we were waiting for a miracle to save the party."

"Taa-daa!" I said, giving her my best jazz hands. "Here's your miracle!"

She laughed as she got up off her chair and came around her desk to give me a high five. "Taa-daa is right."

Just then kids started filing into the room. There were only nine of us in the class, and within a couple of minutes we were all seated.

"All right, everyone." Rabbi Alisha clapped her hands to get everyone's attention. "I have some news for you about the Purim party. It was going to be sad news, but I think Elsie has just turned that around."

"What does that mean?" Jenna asked.

"Well," Rabbi Alisha said. "We were going to have to cancel it, but thanks to Elsie—"

"We're going to make it into a fundraiser!" I blurted.

"That's right," the rabbi said. "But we're going to need some help. Who wants to pitch in?"

Every hand went up.

By the time Sunday school was over, I was sure the party—and the temple—would be saved.

The rabbi was going to email the board that very afternoon to get the official okay for the party. She said everyone would love the idea and that it was just a formality to ask.

Since the food was already booked, the next step was to get tickets made. Mark's parents owned a print shop, and he said they'd donate the tickets.

Other kids said they would talk to their parents about things to donate and ways to help. By the time I got into the back seat of the SUV, my mind was spinning with ideas.

"What has you so bouncy?" Dad asked from the front passenger seat.

"I bet it's brunch," Abba said before I had the chance to reply. "You know how she loves her turkey bacon!"

"Well, that too," I said. Because brunch *was* my favorite. "But also, I am going to save the Purim party. And the temple!"

Abba looked at me in the rearview mirror as he drove out of the parking lot. "What?"

"Well, not *just* me. But it was my idea."

Dad turned around and looked at me. "What was your idea?"

"We're going to turn the party into a fundraiser and sell tickets. That way it won't cost the temple anything and we'll make money."

Dad frowned and then nodded. "Oh. That is a good idea."

"And we're going to make it for everyone," I said. "Like, Grace and her family and anyone from the community who wants to come. Isn't that great? We're going to raise so much money!"

Abba took his eyes off the road long enough to share a weird look with Dad.

"What?" I asked. I hated it when my parents talked without even opening their mouths. I had to guess what they were saying in their heads. The worst part was, I was almost always wrong.

"Just that..." Dad cleared his throat. "I don't know if it's such a great idea to open the party beyond our community."

"What do you mean?" I asked. "It's community outreach. Rabbi Alisha said it was a great idea. She's going to email the board. But everyone will love it. You'll see."

They exchanged another look.

"What now?" I huffed.

"Elsie," Dad said. "It's—"

"You know what?" Abba interrupted. He put a hand on Dad's arm. "It's fine. We're not going to worry."

"Worry? About what?"

They exchanged a third look. I wanted to scream.

"You're right," Dad said. He nodded at Abba and then turned to look at me. He gave me a fake smile. "I'm sure it will be fine. So, Elsie, tell us what you learned at Sunday school today."

They never asked what I learned at Sunday school. And what was with those looks?

They were being so weird.

But why?

Chapter Four

The next day I couldn't wait to get to school. I was excited to see Grace and tell her the great news. She was going to be so pumped about the party!

The second Abba pulled up to the school, I jumped out of the SUV and slammed the door.

Abba put down the window and yelled, "Hey! You forgot something."

"Whoops." I opened the door and reached in for my backpack. "Thanks, Abba."

"That too," he laughed. "But you're forgetting something else. More important than a bag."

I rolled my eyes and came around to the driver's side. When he opened that window, I gave him a big kiss on the cheek. "Have a great day," I said. "Break a leg!"

I said that because Abba worked at a theater. *Break a leg* is what you're supposed to say to actors before they go onstage, instead of *good luck*. He's not an actor, but he says a costume guy is close enough.

"That's better," Abba said. "Who's my favorite daughter?"

"Me, obviously. Who's my favorite father?"

"It had better be me," he said.

"Of course!" I winked.

I always said the same thing to Dad when *he* asked me that question. It was our family joke.

Of course they were both my favorite. Just for different reasons. Abba was outgoing and fun. He liked to dress up and sing and dance. Sometimes he'd put on his old records and we'd have a dance party in our tiny living room.

Dad was quieter and more serious, but in a good way. He loved to sit and watch movies with me. Sometimes we snuggled on the couch and did crosswords together. That was a different kind of fun.

I loved them both more than anything.

"Have a great day, Elsie," Abba said. "Learn lots."

Grace appeared beside me. She waved at Abba as he drove away.

"Hey," I said to my bestie. "How was your Sunday?"

She shrugged. "Church and Sunday school. Same old. You?"

"Same but without church. Come on," I said, starting toward the school. "I have the best news."

By the time we were at our desks in home-room, I had filled Grace in on the plan for the Purim party.

She was really excited about getting to wear her Wonder Woman costume. And she was eager to try hamantaschen.

But mostly she was excited that it was something we'd get to do together.

Which really was the best part.

I had just taken a huge bite of my taco when Dad cleared his throat. "Listen, Elsie…"

Uh-oh. Just those two words told me bad news was coming.

As I chewed, I put my taco down on my plate. Everything fell out of it. Darn tacos. So delicious but such a mess.

I swallowed before I asked, "What is it?"

"It's about the Purim party."

My heart sank. He didn't even have to finish, because I knew what was coming. Operation Purim Fundraiser was a bust.

"Did the board hate the idea?"

"No," Dad said with a snort. "Actually, they loved it. But..." He sighed and shook his head. "You should know that I've told them *I* don't support it."

"*What?*" I glanced at Abba. "What do you mean you don't support it?"

Abba spoke. "Your dad is worried about opening the party up to the whole community."

"But that's the whole point," I said. "We're involving the entire community. And it means Grace can come. We can save the temple!"

"I understand that," Dad said. "But...not all people are open and accepting. I worry that inviting the public is asking for trouble."

He got a sad look on his face. His eyebrows were pinched together, and he was frowning. I knew that face. It meant he was thinking about mean people. People who lashed out at what they didn't understand.

Tears filled my eyes just thinking about what had happened to him only a few months before.

He probably never would have told me. But one night when I'd woken up to use the bathroom, I'd heard them talking. They sounded upset.

When I went into their room and asked what was going on, Dad finally told me. He had lost a big client he'd been about to sign because they'd found out he was gay.

He was sad about it. But Abba was angry. He said a client like that wasn't worth it. But I felt like there was more going on than Dad missing out on a new client.

"What's the rest of the story?" I had asked.

"It's just that…" Dad had sighed. "It got me thinking about when I was in high school. Some kids gave me a hard time for being gay. Some even got physical. I thought I'd left that all behind when I grew up."

"There will always be bullies and haters out there," Abba said sadly. "They don't grow out of it—they just find different ways to show their hate and fear."

It had made me sad. I almost wished I'd never found out. But it had helped me understand why Dad got this way sometimes.

I didn't want him to be afraid to do cool stuff though. Especially when that cool stuff was an epic Purim party.

I picked up my taco, shoving some of the lettuce back in. "Dad, we go to temple all the time. You don't have to worry."

"I know," he said. "We feel safe there, and it's a welcoming community. But we know everyone there."

Abba sighed and looked at Dad. "Are we being paranoid?"

"Maybe," Dad said. "But if it means keeping my family safe…"

"Dad," I said. "Nothing bad's going to happen at temple. Anyway, we've got Abba to protect us."

On cue, Abba flexed his arm muscles. "Darn right you do," he said.

I grinned at him and then turned back to Dad. "You have to channel your Queen Esther and be courageous and fierce."

Dad grunted, but I saw the start of a smile. "Fine. You two have convinced me. I'll be courageous and fierce."

I jumped up out of my chair and gave him a hug and a big kiss on the cheek. "Thank you!"

"Elsie!" he exclaimed. "Did you just smear salsa all over my face?"

Oops. I had. I wiped it off with my thumb. "Whatever. You're my favorite father!"

Abba cleared his throat, pretending to be jealous.

We all laughed.

"Sit down and eat your dinner," Dad said. "Then it's time for homework."

"Ugh," I said. "Maybe you aren't my favorite after all."

Chapter Five

The rest of the week was mostly boring. School, chores and a piano lesson that I wasn't really into.

The only good parts were when Grace and I got to talk about the party. We had three weeks to finish our costumes. It wouldn't be hard, since hers was mostly done and I just needed a crown.

We decided to use the three weeks to learn some new dance moves. We made plans to meet up on

Saturday afternoon at my place to watch YouTube videos for ideas. Abba would help us too.

But first, on Saturday morning, Abba, Dad and I dressed up in our nice clothes and went to temple for Shabbat services.

We always met Bubby and Zaida there. They were Abba's parents (and my grandparents), so we sat together as a family. I sat between Bubby and Abba.

Bubby always whispered the page numbers to me so I could follow along. And most weeks she snuck me a butterscotch. She also smelled nice, like lavender soap.

We sang prayers and followed along with the reading of the Torah. Then Rabbi Alisha did her weekly talk. She was always interesting to listen to, even if I didn't understand everything she said.

Sometimes she'd explain the week's Torah reading so it made more sense. Other times, she talked about our world and how we could make it better. If there was a bar or bat mitzvah, it would take center stage, but she always did a speech and said nice things about the person.

In November, when I would have my bat mitzvah, I'd read from the Torah and she'd do a speech about me. I just hoped we'd be able to have my bat mitzvah here in the temple.

I'd never given much thought to the building I sat in every week and on special occasions. Until now. And now I was determined to save it.

After the service there was always a lunch served in the social hall. Good thing, because the service was long, and by the time we sang "Adon Olam"—the final song—I would be starving.

But first the rabbi would do the weekly announcements.

"I have some great news, everyone," she began this week. "We had thought we would have to cancel our Purim party. But one of our congregants"—she smiled at me—"Elsie Rose-Miller, came up with the fabulous idea to make it into a fundraiser! Packs of tickets to sell will be available from the temple office as of tomorrow. We're hoping to sell out. Hint, hint." She did a big wink, which I guess meant she wanted everyone to sell lots of tickets.

People laughed and then she went on. "And we're opening the event to the community, so please invite all your friends to join us. There will be lots of food, music with dancing and, of course, we'll read the Book of Esther. Wear your best costumes and bring your noisemakers! It promises to be an amazing event!"

I glanced over at Dad. His face was pinched into a frown. He still didn't love the idea of the party being open to everyone.

Abba grabbed my hand and gave it a squeeze. When I looked up at him, he winked.

"What a wonderful idea," Bubby said. She had a big smile on her face. I wondered if she and

Zaida knew about what had happened to Dad. Maybe not.

I was mashing some egg salad on my bagel when Rabbi Alisha came over.

"Shabbat shalom, everyone."

"Shabbat shalom," we replied together.

"Mrs. Rose," she said, looking at Bubby. "I wonder if I could ask you for a favor."

"Oh?" Bubby said after she had carefully wiped her mouth with her napkin.

Rabbi Alisha smiled. "Yes. I was hoping we could use your famous hamantaschen recipe. I thought it would be a good activity for my Sunday schoolers to make some for the party."

Bubby smiled at me. "Of course! What a wonderful idea."

"I have it on my computer," Abba said. "I can print it out and send it with Elsie tomorrow."

"Great," the rabbi said. "You should all be so proud of Elsie. She has such big heart and is so determined."

I grinned at her. "I think you mean I'm fierce and smart."

Everyone laughed.

"That too," Rabbi Alisha said. "But I can't thank you enough for bringing the idea to me. We might have been sunk without it. I just hope we can sell a lot of tickets."

"We will sell a ton of tickets," I assured her. I was certain Abba would sell some to the people at his work. Maybe Dad would too. And Grace plus her parents and two brothers—that was five tickets right there.

Like she had read my mind, Rabbi Alisha looked at my parents. "Should I send Elsie home with a bundle to sell?"

Abba nodded. "Of course. We'll start with twenty."

"We'll take twenty as well," Bubby said. "I'm sure we can sell some to our neighbors."

"Great! Thank you so much," the rabbi said. Then she squeezed my shoulder. "See you tomorrow, Elsie. Don't forget that recipe."

When she had gone to the next table, I gave Abba a look. "Only twenty? I'm sure you can sell more than that," I said. Then I looked at Bubby. "You too. That seniors' home you live in must have a hundred people who would want to come to an epic party."

Zaida snorted as I took a big bite of my bagel.

Abba raised an eyebrow. "You really are fierce and determined, aren't you?"

"And smart," I said with my mouth full. "Don't forget smart."

Chapter Six

As soon as we got home from temple, we all changed out of our nice clothes. Dad wore a suit every day for work, so he was used to it. Abba could never wait to get out of his. He always grumbled until he could put on his worn old jeans.

I couldn't blame him. Ties and stiff shirts looked uncomfortable.

Once they were in their regular clothes, Abba and Dad invited me to go grocery shopping with them.

I was so not interested. I also had other plans. Thankfully.

"Grace is coming over," I said. "We were hoping you'd teach us some dance moves when you get back."

"Oh," Dad said with a frown. "All right. I guess I can show you some—"

"Um. Not to burst your bubble," Abba said as he put a hand on Dad's shoulder, "but I think Elsie was talking to me."

I nodded and tried not to laugh. Dad was not known for his dancing.

He almost looked hurt, so I said, "Maybe Abba can show us *all* some cool dance moves."

Dad rolled his eyes. "Fine. I know what that means." He grabbed his keys and all the shopping bags. "Let's go," he said to Abba.

After they'd left I went into our tiny den and logged into Abba's computer. I found Bubby's famous hamantaschen recipe and clicked *print*. When it was done, I grabbed the page and read it over.

The recipe looked really easy. It gave me an idea. I hadn't done a lot of cooking, but I knew I could make cookies. Especially with the instructions in my hand.

By the time the intercom buzzer rang, I had all the pastry ingredients together on the counter. I'd also taken out a giant glass bowl and the electric mixer.

I pressed the button to open the building's front doors and let Grace in. "Come on up!" I yelled into the intercom.

I waited by our door, staring through the peephole until I heard the *ding* of the elevator. When she stepped off into the hall, I swung open the door.

"Hi! I hope you're ready to bake!"

Grace frowned. "Bake? I thought we were going to dance."

"We'll do that too. First I thought it would be fun to make hamantaschen."

Grace's eyes lit up. "Really? Those cookies you told me about?"

I nodded. "And then we can deliver them tomorrow after Sunday school. Everyone who buys a ticket will get a cookie!"

"Where are we delivering?" Grace asked.

"Everyone in my grandparents' building."

Grace nodded. "That's a good idea."

"Come on." I took her coat and hung it up in the closet while she kicked off her boots.

She followed me into the kitchen. "Where are your dads?"

"Grocery shopping. So boring."

"They don't mind you baking when they're not home?"

Grace's parents were pretty strict, especially about things like using the stove.

Mine weren't as much. At least, I didn't think they were. I'd never actually baked anything by myself before.

I shrugged. "I didn't exactly ask. I'm sure it's fine."

"Okay." Grace went over to the sink to wash her hands. "I help my mom make all our Christmas cookies."

Grace had brought her Christmas cookies to school before the holidays. They were really good. All buttery and sweet. With her help, the hamantaschen would be awesome.

Grace grabbed the recipe off the counter. "Oh, these are so easy. Except…ugh, Elsie. Prunes?" She looked at me and made a face.

"I know," I said, sticking out my tongue. "Some people use prunes for the filling. We won't. My bubby makes them with regular jam."

"Good call. What kind?"

I pulled open the fridge. "Dad is always getting gift baskets, so we probably have every kind of jam you can imagine." I started pulling out jars and handing them to Grace. "Apricot, strawberry, orange marmalade…"

"Let's do some apricot and some strawberry. Marmalade is too sour for cookies."

"My bubby does apricot." I closed the fridge. I frowned at the jars on the counter. "But apricot and strawberry are so boring. I want to do something fun and exciting."

"What kind of jam is fun and exciting?" Grace asked.

"Hmm. What would Queen Esther put in *her* hamantaschen?"

Grace shrugged. "What do I know about Queen Esther?"

Good point. I didn't know much about Queen Esther either. Other than that she was fierce and smart.

"Come on," I said. I led Grace back to Abba's computer. We googled *Queen Esther* and *food*. We learned that in Queen Esther's time, things like dates, pomegranates and poppy seeds were popular foods. I was sad that Queen Esther never got to eat Oreos.

"We don't have any of those things," I said when we got back to the kitchen.

"So…apricot jam?" Grace said.

"We can do better than boring old jam." I looked in the cupboard. "Oh, wait. We have this."

"Everything bagel sprinkles?" Grace laughed. "I doubt Queen Esther had that."

"You don't know," I said. I put the jar on the counter. "Maybe she invented it. She was supersmart. And it has poppy seeds in it." I looked at the ingredients. "And sesame seeds too. What's not to like?"

Grace gave me a suspicious look. I turned back to the fridge.

"What else, what else," I said. "Oh hey, this is kind of like jam." I pulled out a jar and showed it to Grace.

"Hot pepper jelly?"

"It's zingy. That would be good with the bagel sprinkles." I put it down on the counter next to the jar of seasoning. I turned back toward the fridge. I leaned in to get to all the jars in the back. "Oh, how about this? It's basically jam."

"Pickle relish?" Grace hooted with laughter. "Elsie! That's ridiculous!"

I laughed. "Queen Esther wouldn't have thought so. She would have said it was *original*. Oh, wait. Didn't that website say they ate a lot of olives back then?" I grabbed the bottle of black-olive spread that Dad mixed into his pasta.

"Elsie," Grace said in her sternest voice. "You can't make olive-paste cookies. They would be so gross!"

That just made me more determined. "I bet Queen Esther ate olive cookies. You can't argue with history, Grace. Even if it's gross."

She rolled her eyes. "Whatever, Elsie."

"Come on," I said, slamming the fridge door closed. "We need to start with the dough. Grab the flour. I'll beat the eggs."

"All right," she said. She pushed her sleeves up her arms. "If you're sure."

"So sure," I said. "Just wait and see, Grace. Our hamantaschen are going to be amazing."

Chapter Seven

"You know what's amazing, Elsie?" Grace said. "That I let you talk me into eating a relish cookie! So. Gross."

"You barely even had a bite," I said.

"Trust me, it was enough." She dropped the rest of her hamantaschen into the trash can. "And I don't see you finishing your olive-paste cookie."

"Uh, Grace," I said. "Everyone knows you're supposed to eat slowly. That's how you enjoy your food." At least, that's what Dad liked to say when I was scarfing french fries.

Still, Grace wasn't wrong. I hadn't actually taken a bite of the center part with the olive filling yet. I wasn't so sure I wanted to either.

Now that the cookies were baked, I was having second thoughts about my special flavors. The kitchen smelled weird. Maybe boring old jam would have been better.

The relish ones looked like they were filled with boogers. I didn't say that though, or Grace would never have tried one.

Now she was staring at me, waiting.

"Stop gawking at me," I said. "It's delicious. Obviously."

"Then take another bite."

"I will," I said.

But I didn't. I just stood there.

She tilted her head. "Were you planning on taking that bite next week? Because I've got time."

Queen Esther might be fierce, but Grace Jackson was stubborn. She was going to stare at me forever if she had to. I took a nibble. "Mmm, so…olive-y! Delicious!"

Grace clucked and crossed her arms. "Please. How about a bite of the center? You know, where the olive stuff is?"

"I did!" But I hadn't.

Just then the front door opened, and I heard the jingle of keys.

Thank goodness!

"We're home," Abba called out.

"I'd better go help," I said to Grace as I slid the rest of the cookie back onto the baking sheet. I started toward the front door. She made a noise but followed me.

"Hi, Grace," Dad said as Abba beamed a big smile at my best friend. "What am I smelling?"

"We baked hamantaschen!" I peeked inside the shopping bags Dad had put down. Vegetables. How boring.

"You baked?" Abba's eyes lit up. "Wow, really?"

I nodded. "I printed out Bubby's recipe. We thought we could take some to Bubby and Zaida's building tomorrow. We can give them out to help sell Purim party tickets."

"Great idea," Abba said. He started toward the kitchen with his bags.

Dad hung up his keys on the hook by the door. "You're really determined to make this party a success, aren't you?"

I nodded and looped my arm through Grace's. "We both are. It's going to be awesome, and we'll get to save the temple. Together."

Grace held up her other hand and we fist-bumped. "Together."

"Elsie!" Abba hollered from the kitchen. "Can you come in here, please?"

Dad's eyebrows went up high on his head. "That doesn't sound good. Did you girls make a big mess in the kitchen?"

Well, yes. But I had a feeling that was not what Abba was yelling about.

Abba almost never yelled. *Uh-oh.*

I glanced at Grace. Her lips were pressed together hard. She was trying not to laugh.

"Elsie!" Abba boomed.

I hurried into the kitchen. Abba was hunched over the trash, spitting food into the can. It was black. One of the olive hamantaschen, I guessed.

He did not look happy.

"What's going on?" Dad asked. He looked from Abba to me. Then back to Abba. "You okay?"

"No," Abba said. "I mean, I'll live, but…" He made a face and then pulled open the fridge door and grabbed a soda. He opened the can and took a long drink. Finally he said, "I *thought* I was eating a poppy seed hamantaschen."

"We don't have any poppy seeds," Dad said. He gave me a confused look.

Abba glared at Dad. "I just learned that the hard way. What *was* that, Elsie?"

"Uh, olive paste?"

There was a long silence.

Dad snorted. "You made olive hamantaschen?"

I shrugged. "In Queen Esther's time, they ate a lot of olives. So it's like history. Anyway, I thought it would be different than boring old jam."

"Oh, it was different, all right," Abba said. He took another big drink of the soda.

"And the others?" Dad said, pointing at the tray.

"Uh, the green ones are relish. The others are red pepper jelly with everything bagel sprinkles."

"Inventive," Dad said. "Onions and garlic are just what I look for in a cookie!"

"Want to try one?" I asked hopefully.

Dad held up a hand. "Hard pass."

"I told her, Mr. Rose-Miller," Grace said. "I told her they'd be gross. She wouldn't listen."

"Some things you just have to learn on your own," Dad said with a smile. Then, a second later, he frowned. "Wait a minute. You didn't use all my good olive tapenade, did you?"

I cringed. "Um. Not all of it."

Dad rolled his eyes. "Elsie."

"You love that stuff so much, Paul," Abba said. "Maybe *you'll* like the cookies."

"Still a hard pass," Dad said, but he was laughing.

"Let's get these groceries put away and then we can clean up," Abba said. "And by 'we,' I mean you girls. Then I seem to remember there was supposed to be dancing."

I gave Abba a hug. "Yes, please."

"Groceries first," Dad said. He pulled open the fridge and started putting stuff away.

"You know what?" Abba said. His face was all scrunched up. "While you all put everything away, I'm going to go brush my teeth."

"It can't be that bad!" I said.

Abba gave me a look. "Did you eat one?"

"Yes!" I said at the same moment as Grace said, "No!"

Abba rolled his eyes. "I love you, Elsie. But I'm going to have nightmares about that cookie."

I gave him another hug. "You're my favorite," I whispered into his shirt.

"Uh-huh." He chuckled as he ended the hug. "Let me go brush my teeth. And use some mouthwash. And maybe a power washer." He shivered and left the kitchen.

I felt bad.

But I was secretly glad it wasn't me who had eaten the cookie.

Chapter Eight

Abba dropped me off early for Sunday school the next day. When I got into our classroom, I gave Mark a little wave on my way to Rabbi Alisha's desk.

She looked up from her book and smiled. "Good morning, Elsie."

I handed her the folded recipe. "Here you go."

She thanked me and looked down, unfolding the page. "This looks like a much-loved recipe," she said. "Please tell your grandmother thank you for me."

That's when I noticed all the food splotches on the paper. Relish juice, a smear of olive paste. Even a sesame seed stuck in the middle.

"Uh, I actually just printed that out yesterday. My friend Grace and I made some." *Well, tried to make some*, I didn't say.

Rabbi Alisha's eyebrows went up. "Oh, how wonderful!"

I shook my head. "No. Not wonderful. Pretty gross, actually."

"Oh no. What happened?"

I shrugged. "I thought jam would be boring. I went a different way."

"Oh?" She looked like she was trying not to smile.

I sighed. "Let's just say olive paste doesn't make for good hamantaschen. Neither does green relish."

Rabbi Alisha coughed. Actually, I'm pretty sure she laughed but covered it up with a cough.

Then she cleared her throat. "No, I wouldn't think so. Although I applaud your creativity."

"Yeah, that's what Dad said."

She smiled. "Anyway, we will be making ours for the party with traditional fillings."

"Probably a good thing." I sighed. "But I wanted to take them around to my grandparents' building. I had thought we could give them out and sell tickets to the party."

"That's a great idea. And you know about the practice of delivering mishloach manot on Purim. The giving out of baskets of food to ensure everyone has enough. So offering hamantaschen with the tickets would be very appropriate."

"Are we making some today?" I asked.

Rabbi Alisha shook her head. "I'm sorry, no. We only have enough supplies to make them for the party in two weeks."

"Oh."

"But I do have your tickets." She picked up an envelope from a stack on her desk and handed it to me. *Rose-Miller* was typed on the front. "Mark's family was so generous to print out the tickets for us. Here are the ones for your dads."

"Thanks."

"And here's some for your grandparents." She handed me another envelope with *Rose* on it.

"What about for me?" I looked for another envelope but didn't see any other Rose-Millers.

"I want to make sure everyone gets some to start with. But if you and your fathers need more, let me know."

I planned to let her know. I was hoping to sell dozens of tickets in my grandparents' building alone!

When class began a few minutes later, Rabbi Alisha told the class about the tickets, handing out the rest to people whose families had requested them.

She also told us how she'd gotten a phone call from the caterer. When they'd heard the party would be a fundraiser, they'd offered to give the temple a big discount to help.

"Between that and us baking the hamantaschen ourselves, we're going to save a bundle," Rabbi Alisha said. "We've already sold tickets too. When I came in this morning, there were several phone messages and emails. I bet they're still coming in!"

She was so excited. I was too. We all were. It was a great feeling to be doing something that would be fun and helpful. Plus I was going to get to do it with my best friend. And we would get to wear costumes. Could anything be more fun? I doubted it.

Kendra stuck her hand up high. She was bouncing in her seat.

"Yes, Kendra?"

"Well, you know how my mom owns the party store? She wants to donate all the decorations. Streamers, balloons, noisemakers—whatever. She said you should call her or pop into the store to talk about it."

Rabbi Alisha clasped her hands together. "Oh my goodness. That is so wonderful." She took a deep breath. "You all are overwhelming me today."

Sidney lifted his hand. "My parents said they would donate some door prizes. That means raffle prizes, not actual doors for people to win. I asked."

We all laughed.

Sidney's family owned a card and gift shop.

"That would be amazing, Sidney. Thank you," Rabbi Alisha said. She took a deep breath and let it out slowly. "So…that doesn't leave much for us to pay for. The cantor said he'd be DJ for the evening. Which means that other than food costs, most of the money we raise can go directly back to the temple.

"We might just do this, kids," she said with a big smile. "We might just save this place."

"Yeah, we will!" I said, doing a fist pump into the air.

Everyone joined in.

"Yes!" said Mark.

"Of course we will!" shouted Kendra.

"Yeah!" Hanna said.

"You know what?" Rabbi Alisha said. "With you kids on the job, I have no doubt."

She took another long breath. "Okay. Enough of that for now. Time for this week's lesson. Since it's just over two weeks away and we all have Purim on the brain, I thought we'd discuss the story of Esther."

We'd learned all this before—like, every year. So while she talked, I kept thinking about things to donate and even more ways to make the party awesome. We were totally going to save the temple.

Chapter Nine

After Sunday school and brunch, my dads and I returned to our apartment. I was excited for Grace to come over so we could go to my grandparents' building to sell tickets.

But the second I got through the front door, I knew something was up.

"What's that smell?" I asked. It was familiar. Almost like the baking smell from the day before, except good. Really good.

Abba smiled as he hung up his keys. "While you were at Sunday school, Dad and I baked hamantaschen."

"What? For real?"

I didn't wait for his answer. I rushed into the kitchen. There, on cooling racks on the counter, were tons of beautiful triangular cookies. They looked perfect. They smelled even better. Way better than the ones I'd made.

I'd just eaten a huge stack of pancakes, but I still began to drool. There were four different fillings—orange, yellow, black and red.

"But *I* wanted to make them," I said.

"You can help us make the next batch," Dad said.

"We made them for you to take to your grandparents' building. We liked your idea of giving them out with the tickets."

"Can I have one?" My hand hovered over an orange one. I was pretty sure it was apricot.

Abba shook his head. "We made them to give out, Elsie."

My hand got closer to the cookie, but I was careful not to touch it. "Please, Abba? I should get to try at least one."

I was going to say that he'd gotten to eat one that I'd made. But reminding him of the olive hamantaschen wasn't going to get me any bonus points. Or a cookie.

"Let her have one," Dad said. "Don't be cruel."

"You know what's cruel?" Abba said. "That olive hamantaschen I ate yesterday. I told you—nightmares." He shivered.

So much for him not remembering.

"Aaaabbaaaaaa," I said, my fingers twitching closer to the treat. Still not touching it, though. "Pleeeeeease!"

"Fine," he sighed. "You may have one. Grace may also have one when she gets here."

He wasn't even done speaking before I'd grabbed the cookie. I took a huge bite.

"Mmm. So good," I said.

Fruity and sweet. Apricot, just as I'd hoped.

Not even a hint of olive.

When Grace came over, she was impressed with the cookies. When I told her she could have one, she was even more impressed. She chose the biggest strawberry-filled one. It was gone in two bites.

But when I saw her staring hopefully at an apricot one, I reminded her the cookies were to help us sell tickets for the party.

"Fine," she said with a big sigh. I understood because I wanted another one too.

I got out the little paper treat bags left over from my last birthday. We put one hamantaschen into each. Then we tied each bag up with blue ribbon leftover from Hanukkah.

"Uh-oh," Grace said when we were halfway done. She frowned at me. "I broke one. What should I do?"

"We can't give a broken cookie to someone," I told her. "That's unprofessional."

There was only one thing we could do. We shared it. It was lemon. So good. We accidentally (truly) broke two more—one strawberry and one apricot—before we were finished packaging them all.

Mistakes were delicious!

My grandparents' building was only about six blocks away, so Grace and I bundled up to walk there. We put the cookies and tickets in a tote bag and left my building. We practiced our dancing on the way. Neither of us were great dancers, but at least we had some new moves.

The day before, after he'd brushed his teeth and complained some more about how I'd tried to poison him with the olive hamantaschen, Abba had put on some music and shown us a few new routines. Even Dad had joined in. The four of us had had the tiniest dance party ever in our little living room. It was a small party, but it was still super fun.

Grace and I still had time to practice. We were determined to be the best dancers at the party!

When we got to my grandparents' building, Bubby buzzed us in. We took the elevator to their floor and walked down the long hall to their door.

Bubby answered when I knocked. "Hello, girls. Take your boots off. You both look like you could use some hot chocolate to warm up after your walk."

"Yes, please!" Grace and I said together.

I hung the tote bag on the closet door handle. We took off our coats and boots and followed Bubby into the kitchen. We sat at the table while she put on the kettle.

I told her how we were going to sell tickets around the building. She wrote a list of the apartments where she thought people would be most likely to buy some.

While we waited for the water to boil, she arranged some of her own home-baked cookies on a plate. They weren't hamantaschen but were just as good.

"Tell me about your Purim costumes," Bubby said.

"Grace is going to be Wonder Woman," I said.

Grace nodded. "Fierce and smart. Just like Gal Gadot."

"Oh, I love her." Bubby brought over the cookies and sat down with us. "I'll see any movie she's in."

I reached for a cookie. "Us too."

"And your costume?" Bubby asked me.

"Queen Esther. Also fierce and smart."

"Another worthy role model," Bubby said. "I presume Abba is making it for you?"

"Yep. I haven't seen it, but it's going to be green velvet. And I got this cool green and gold scarf to go with it at the thrift shop. I just need a crown. But I might make it, if I can't find a good one."

Bubby was looking at me with a smile on her face.

"What?" I wiped my mouth with my hand. Maybe I had crumbs stuck to my face.

"Come with me," she said. She turned off the stove under the kettle, and we followed her into her bedroom.

I looked at Grace, but she shrugged.

Bubby opened her closet and disappeared inside. We could hear her rummaging around.

"I need to get rid of so much," she said. Her voice was muffled by all the clothes. "There it is."

"What are you looking for, Bubby?"

She didn't answer, but a minute later she came out with a belt. It was gold and shimmered in the light. "Maybe this will go with your dress."

"Yes!" I said, reaching for it. "It's perfect. I totally love it."

"That'll go so well with the scarf," Grace said. "It has gold just like that."

Bubby smiled at me.

"Were you Queen Esther once for Purim?" I asked.

Bubby laughed. "No."

"Was it for Halloween?" Grace asked.

Bubby smiled at her. "Not a costume. This is the kind of thing I wore every day. Everyone wore things like that back then. Gold, shiny fabrics. Lots of belts and accessories. Frosty makeup. It was a different time."

"Oh," I said. I wrapped the belt around my waist. It was too big, but Abba could fix it. "So this was cool when you were young?"

Bubby made a face. "Something like that. I don't know why I never got rid of it." She shrugged. "Maybe for this moment. Now it's yours."

"Thank you." I gave her a hug. "I'm going to wear it when we go to sell tickets. Maybe it will make people want to dress up too."

"I'm sure it will," Bubby said. She shut her closet door. "Now let's go see about that hot chocolate."

Chapter Ten

We sold out of my twenty tickets almost right away. We returned to Bubby and Zaida's to drop off the money and get their batch to sell. Bubby was impressed. She told us we must be great salespeople. I wasn't going to argue.

After a bathroom break, Bubby handed over the envelope with their tickets, and Grace and I started back out.

About ten minutes later Grace took a bite of hamantaschen. "This is so easy!" she said as she chewed. The last lady we'd sold tickets to hadn't wanted any cookies. She'd said she couldn't eat sweets and that we should have them. Who were we to argue?

Selling tons of tickets *and* getting to keep the cookies for ourselves? Did it get any better? I didn't think so. Community outreach was awesome.

"I know," I said. "We've sold almost all of them!" I reached into the tote for another cookie. "Just four tickets left."

"We'll sell them in no time." Grace brushed the last of the crumbs from her hands. "What's the next address?"

I glanced at the list. "There aren't any left on Bubby's list. We got them all!"

"Should we go back?" Grace asked. "There were a few on the fifth floor who weren't home. We can try them again."

I looked down the hall. There were four doors on the third floor that we hadn't knocked on. "Let's keep going here. I'm sure we'll sell the rest." It would be so amazing if we sold them all in just one day!

Grace nodded. She was as determined as I was. "Oh hey," she said as we walked down the hall. "I was thinking. My auntie Ally volunteers for a community TV station. She's been taping some sports events, but I could call her and see if she'll do a story on the fundraiser. What do you think?"

"What do I think?!" I threw my arms around Grace and gave her a huge hug. "I think it's the best idea ever!"

We turned, finding ourselves in front of apartment 3C. Grace knocked on the door.

We heard some shuffling and then the door swung open. It was an old man with a big belly, wearing a plaid shirt that looked like it was about to pop a few buttons. He had long, bushy eyebrows and thick glasses. He was frowning.

I suddenly wished we hadn't knocked on the door. The look on Grace's face said she was thinking the same thing. This man wasn't smiling or happy to see us the way all the other seniors had been. This man acted like we'd interrupted his nap.

I thought about running away. But it was a long way to the elevator. Plus outreach meant engaging the community. Even the people that weren't like us. That's what Rabbi Alisha always said.

"What do you want?" the man growled.

I cleared my throat and gave him my best smile. "Hello, sir," I said. "We're selling tickets for the Temple Beth El Purim fundraiser."

"And each ticket comes with a free hamantaschen," Grace added.

"Temple what? A free *what*?"

"Temple Beth El. It's a fundraiser for the synagogue, sir," I said. "Hamantaschen is a type of cookie." I pulled one out of the tote bag and offered it to him. He didn't move except to sneer at the bag in my hand.

His bushy eyebrows went up and then down like caterpillars on a branch. It would have been funny if he hadn't been glaring at us. "You want *me* to give *Jews* money?"

Oh.

The way he'd said *Jews* sounded...mean.

"Let's go, Grace," I said, grabbing her arm. "Sorry, sir, we didn't mean to bother you."

Grace wasn't done trying though.

"Yes, sir. It's to help the synagogue," she said. "A fundraiser. But it'll be a really fun party. Everyone can go—it's not just for Jewish people. I'm going, and I'm not Jewish."

He made a rude noise. "You expect me to go to a party for a bunch of *Jews*?" Then he narrowed his eyes at Grace. "And you. Who let *you* in the building?"

When he said *you* I knew he was talking about Grace being Black. And he'd said it the same way he'd said *Jews*.

"Come on, Grace." I pulled her down the hallway away from the man.

The man yelled after us, "You rotten kids shouldn't be running around the building. I'm calling the cops if you don't get out of here!"

Forget waiting for the elevator. We needed to get away from him as fast as we could. "Stairs!" I yelled. We ran and slammed open the big door to the stairwell. I wanted to go up to Bubby and Zaida's floor, but we could only go down, because the stairwell doors were locked. We hurried to the ground floor and came out into the lobby, huffing and puffing.

"What just happened?" Grace said between breaths. "Was he for real?"

"That man was the worst. Racist and antisemitic and...ugh! What a jerk!"

"The absolute worst. A total jerk," Grace said, her voice cracking. "I'm surprised he didn't start calling us awful names."

"I know." Tears pooled in my eyes as I thought about the mean names he might have used. "I'm sorry, Grace."

She wiped away a tear of her own and gave me a hug. "It's not your fault, Elsie. He is the one with the problem."

"Yeah. Still..." I said.

"I just don't understand how people can hate people they don't even know."

"Me neither," I said. "Especially awesome people like us. We even offered him cookies!"

"Not like he deserved them." Grace shrugged and sniffled. "He's probably mean to everyone."

"Come on. Let's go back up to Bubby and Zaida's. We sold enough today, I guess."

She nodded. "He kind of ruined everything. I know you wanted to sell all the tickets."

"No," I said, grabbing her hand and tugging on it until she looked at me. "We did a good job. Don't let one crabby old man ruin everything. We sold most of our tickets. We are going to save the synagogue, and we got to eat a lot of hamantaschen."

She nodded.

I went on, "And we're best friends and we're doing it all together. That's what really matters."

Grace gave me a half smile and squeezed my hand before she let it go. "I guess. It's just…"

"I know," I said. "Come on. Let's go get our stuff." I led her over to the elevator and pushed the button. We got on and held our breath as the elevator flew past the third floor. No one got on there, which was a relief.

We didn't tell Bubby about the crabby old man. But she knew something was up and kept asking what was wrong. We just told her everything was fine.

I gave her back the four remaining tickets and the rest of the hamantaschen too. After *her* cookies, the hot chocolate and all the hamantaschen, my tummy wasn't feeling so great.

Neither was my heart.

Even with my best friend at my side, the walk home felt long and cold.

Chapter Eleven

Grace left me at the door to my apartment building. She said she needed to go home and finish her homework before the weekend was over. Really, I think she was just sad like I was and needed to be alone.

But before she left, she gave me a hug that we both needed.

I was going to tell my parents about the mean old man when I got up to our apartment. They always said I could tell them anything, no matter what.

But when I walked in the door, they asked how many tickets we had sold. When I told them, they were so excited and proud of what we'd done, I didn't want to ruin their mood the way the man had ruined mine and Grace's. So I pushed what had happened out of my head. Instead I thought about all the good that had come from the day. We'd sold a ton of tickets and eaten plenty of treats, and I'd gotten a cool gold belt.

When I pulled the belt out of my tote bag to show them, Abba laughed. "Wow, that's…shiny. Did she buy it for you?"

"No," I said. "It's hers. She said back in the day everyone wore stuff like this."

"Back in the day, huh?" Dad was smiling. "What was she keeping it for? A mah-jongg tournament in her building? I wonder what else she has in her closet."

"I don't know," Abba said. "But I'm going to find out. I can't believe she hid treasures like this from me!"

Abba loved clothes and playing dress-up. He said that's what had made him want to be a costume designer in the first place.

"Maybe she was saving it for me," I said. "For the costume she somehow knew I would wear someday. You know, the costume I haven't seen yet," I reminded Abba. Because I couldn't wait. Especially now that I had the belt, sandals, mask and scarf to go with it.

Abba smiled. "Next Saturday we can go pick it up after temple. We're almost done with it."

"*We*?" I looked at Dad, but he just shrugged. "Who is *we*?"

Abba's smile turned into a giant grin. "I may have asked Bella if she'd help."

"Bella?" I gasped. "Really?"

When he nodded, I threw my arms around him in a huge bear hug. Bella was the master seamstress who worked at the theater. She didn't just make all the costumes from scratch, she sewed gems and glitter onto costumes by hand. Her costumes were more than just clothes. Each one was a piece of art.

If she had worked on my Queen Esther dress, it wasn't just going to be great. It was going to be amazing.

"Thank you, Abba," I said, squishing him harder. "This party is going to be the best ever."

Tuesday night I was all alone in the apartment. Abba was at work, and Dad was downstairs in the gym, working out.

I'd decided to use the quiet time to work on my costume. I still didn't have my Queen Esther crown made. I was sitting at the kitchen table to sketch it out. I wasn't sure yet how I was going to make a crown, but I would figure it out.

Abba said all good costume designers draw out their plans first. Even if you're not good at drawing, he said, putting it down on paper will help you see the design.

I had only just started when my pencil broke. *Figures.*

I went into the den to find a pencil sharpener and saw a folder on Dad's desk. It said *Temple Beth El Financials.*

My heart sank.

Maybe I shouldn't have looked, but it wasn't like I could help it. And Dad hadn't told me *not* to look. There was no TOP SECRET sticker on it or anything. Still, I glanced over my shoulder before I flipped the folder open with my finger.

The top page said *balance sheet,* with a bunch of words and numbers that didn't make sense to me. I mostly ignored it, even though the numbers were really big.

But as I looked at the pages underneath, I saw that they were bills. Big bills. For roof repairs, carpet cleaning, plumbing and a whole new air conditioning system. Each bill was thousands and thousands of dollars. More money than I could even imagine.

We were charging twenty-five dollars for each Purim party ticket and then would be selling raffle tickets for the donated prizes. Would that be enough?

The temple was probably doomed. What then?

I didn't want to have my bat mitzvah at a funeral home!

The one thing I did know? Everything really was riding on this party.

Chapter Twelve

It had been the longest week ever. I was supposed to focus on school. But when Grace and I got together on Wednesday after class to study for our math test, we just couldn't. All we could talk about was the party. Our costumes for the party, what we would eat at the party and, most important, how we had to make it the most successful party ever.

I had told Grace about the bills I'd seen on Dad's desk. She'd spoken to her auntie Ally about doing a story, and Ally had promised to call the rabbi.

When we were done talking, we practiced our dancing.

We did study. A little. Especially when Dad came into the room and reminded us that dancing was not going to help us do well in math. He made a face that meant he wasn't joking.

We did well enough on the test, though. Grace got a B+ and I got a B.

Saturday—costume-reveal day—finally came. I could barely sit still in my chair at temple. Bubby had already whispered at me twice to stop fidgeting, but I couldn't help it. I couldn't wait to see my costume!

The service dragged on.

And on.

And on.

Even Rabbi's talk seemed longer than usual. I sort of tuned out until she started her update on the party. She thanked all the members who had donated door prizes and auction items. Then she thanked everyone who had been selling tickets. She looked right at me when she said that part. I wondered if I'd sold more than anyone else.

"And," she said, looking so excited, "we've been contacted by a local journalist who wants to do a feature on the event for a community TV piece."

She smiled at me. The journalist had to be Grace's aunt.

The rabbi continued, "Don't forget that if you need more tickets, pick them up at the temple office. We're less than two weeks away! Thank you again to everyone. Shabbat shalom."

Finally! That meant the service was over. After we ate lunch, we got into the car, and my dads took me to Abba's theater.

Even though Abba takes Saturdays off, it's actually the theater's busiest day. There are two shows on Saturdays—a matinee in the afternoon and an evening one.

So when we got there, there were tons of people inside. Some were hanging out and talking, drinking from giant water bottles. A few were in their practice clothes, stretching, and a group was rehearsing a song from the show (*Fiddler on the Roof*, which was my absolute favorite—I'd seen it three times already).

As Abba led us to the costume shop, everyone greeted us. High fives and lots of smiles. Everyone loved Abba.

When we got inside, I took a deep breath through my nose. The theater smelled like no other place I'd ever been. The scent was a mix of the lemon polish they used on the wood in the front of house (where the audience sat), a touch of mustiness from the old costumes, air freshener, gym shoe and adventure, all rolled into one. It was one of my favorite smells in the world.

I'd been there before, of course, but on every visit I noticed something new. The costume shop was packed with a million things. Not just clothes but wigs, hats, tights, shoes—everything you could imagine.

One day I was going to get Abba to bring me and Grace here so we could all play the most epic game of dress-up.

But today was about my Queen Esther costume.

"Elsie!" Bella yelled when she saw us. She jumped up from her sewing machine and rushed over. She grabbed me and hugged me hard. I laughed and hugged her back. She was my favorite person at the theater. Besides Abba, of course.

Bella had worked at the theater forever. She was an older lady with glasses on a chain around her neck. She always smelled nice, like spring flowers and fabric.

She gave me a kiss on the cheek and then used her thumb to wipe off the lipstick mark she'd left behind. "I'm so happy to see you! Look how big you've gotten."

I smiled at her. "Thank you for working on my costume."

"Who else?" She grabbed my hand. "Come."

She led me to her office in the back and shut us in, just the two of us.

Two minutes later I was looking at Queen Esther in the mirror.

"Bella!" I turned to face her, fighting tears of happiness. "It's perfect. It's…it's the fiercest and most beautiful thing I've ever worn!"

She plucked a loose thread from my sleeve. "I'm so glad you like it."

"Like it? I adore it!" I spun back to the mirror because I couldn't stop looking. I smoothed my hands down the soft, fuzzy velvet. It fit perfectly, like I'd known it would.

"I have a scarf and gold belt and sandals that will go perfectly with this. And the mask I made too. I'm going to be the best Queen Esther there's ever been! Since the first one, I mean."

Bella laughed. "Wait. There's one more thing."

"More?" I couldn't even imagine what more she could have sewn for me.

She opened a cabinet and pulled out something wrapped in tissue paper. I held my breath as she carefully pulled the tissue away.

"Bella!" I gasped.

"I had one of the prop people make it."

It was a crown. The most beautiful gold crown with green emeralds on it. If I'd sketched for a million years, I never would have come up with something half as perfect.

Now I did cry. I couldn't help it. "It's beautiful, Bella. Thank you so much."

She lifted it and put it on my head. "There. I crown you Queen Esther."

The costume made me feel strong and fierce. I wished I could wear it every day.

I looked in the mirror. I stood tall, shoulders back, chin up. I got how even though her life had been in terrible danger, Queen Esther had mustered all her courage. She had been so brave and had saved her people from the evil man who wanted to kill them all.

Chapter Thirteen

Finally it was Thursday, the day of the party.

I woke up early, surprised I'd slept at all. I snuggled under my blankets, thinking about the night before. Dad and I had helped decorate the temple's hall with all the stuff Kendra and her mom had brought over.

We had taped up streamers and hung signs and banners. We'd blown up and arranged balloons.

We'd moved all the tables around, making room for a dance floor and a place for the food. We'd laid the tablecloths and arranged noisemakers and colorful confetti on every table.

By the time we were done, it was late, but our work was so worth it. The room was colorful and sparkly. Perfect for what was going to be the best Purim party ever.

I stretched and looked at the costume hanging on the back of my bedroom door.

I loved every part of it. The green velvet dress that was more beautiful than I could have imagined. The crown that had been made just for me and was a million times better than a junky dollar-store one. The fancy scarf I'd bought, my grandmother's matching belt, the mask I'd made myself and even the sandals—every element was perfect.

I wanted to put everything on but couldn't risk getting the dress dirty before the big event.

The big event that was tonight! Just hours away!

Dad had said I could take the day off school. Not just because of the party, though. It was so Abba and I could give out the Purim baskets.

Giving baskets of treats to people in the community was an important part of the Purim holiday. Maybe even more important than the party, Rabbi Alisha had said.

My Sunday school class had baked tons of hamantaschen (with regular jam filling) in the temple kitchen on the weekend. We'd put half aside for the party and all worked together to put the rest into the baskets. We had other goodies to put in too.

Each basket had gotten five cookies, a package of trail mix, an apple, a pear, two oranges and five pieces of chocolate. Then the rabbi and everyone in our class had signed Happy Purim tags, attaching each to a basket with a pretty ribbon tied in a bow.

By the end of Sunday school, the temple's giant walk-in fridge had been filled with baskets. Rabbi Alisha had dismissed us, but only after telling us how proud she was of our hard work.

Abba would take me out this morning to hand out our baskets. We'd deliver half to people in my grandparents' building. We'd take the rest to a women's shelter.

Then Abba would drop me off at home and go to work for a few hours, until it was time to get ready for the party.

I'd have the afternoon to catch up on my homework since I'd be missing school. At least, that's what I was supposed to do. I didn't really think homework would be happening. I'd be too excited about the party. But I wasn't going to tell Abba that.

When we pulled up to the temple to collect our baskets, I knew right away that something was wrong. Not just because of the three police cars in the parking lot. Or the six police officers standing by the front door. Or by Rabbi Alisha standing there in her coat and hat, frowning. Her face was all red. She was obviously upset. Her arms were crossed, and she kept nodding as one of the officers talked to her

Those things were all part of it, of course.

But when Abba turned off the car and swore? That's when I knew something was really, really wrong.

Abba *never* swore.

"Abba?" My heart began to race. My whole body filled with dread. Whatever this was, it was bad.

"Stay here." He got out of the car and started walking quickly toward the group. That's when

I saw the red, spray-painted symbols on the temple doors.

I knew what they were. Swastikas.

And they meant that whoever had painted them hated Jewish people. Jewish people like me. Like my parents. My grandparents. People who came to Sabbath services every week. Rabbi Alisha and everyone in my Sunday school class.

I couldn't help but think of that old man from my grandparents' building. Could he have done this? Could he have done it to get back at me for bothering him about the tickets? Was he so mean that he would spray-paint hateful symbols on my temple? I couldn't imagine *anyone* being so mean that they would want people to feel hated.

But he'd been so awful, I couldn't help but wonder.

Most of the time I was a kid who listened to her parents.

Not today. I opened the door and got out of the car.

Chapter Fourteen

I walked right up to the group. "What's happening?"

Abba turned around when he heard me. "Elsie. I told you to stay in the car."

"It's my temple too. I want to know what happened."

I looked at Rabbi Alisha. Her face was still red. I could tell she had been crying. No, actually, she was still crying. She held out her arms, and when

I stepped closer, she pulled me into a hug. "I'm so sorry you have to see this," she said. "The temple has been vandalized."

"Do you know who it was?" I asked.

She pulled back and shook her head. "We looked at the security tapes, but all we could see were dark figures."

"Could one of them have been an old man?" I asked. "With bushy eyebrows and a big belly?"

Abba spun toward me. "You know who did this?"

I took a breath. "I don't know. Maybe?"

One of the policemen, who held a notebook and pen, stepped toward me. "I'm Officer Kent. Can you please tell me anything you might know? Even if it seems small or unrelated."

I glanced up at Abba. "That day when Grace and I sold tickets in Bubby and Zaida's building?"

He nodded. "Yes...go on."

"We knocked on a door on the third floor. An old man answered, and he was really mean."

Abba frowned. "What did he say?"

"I don't know, just...we got the feeling he didn't like Jewish people." I glanced at the officer. He was Black. "Or Black people," I added. "I'm sorry."

"You have nothing to be sorry for," the officer said.

Rabbi Alisha gave my shoulder a squeeze.

"Did this man threaten you at all?" Officer Kent asked.

"Not really. He was just mean. He said he was going to call the cops if we didn't get out of the building." Tears began to fall from my eyes. "He said he wasn't going to go to a party full of Jews."

Abba pulled me into his side. I put my arm around his waist and mashed my face into his coat.

"The people on the security footage seemed young," Rabbi Alisha said. "I assumed it was teenagers."

"That man probably wasn't the person who did this." The officer turned to Abba. "But we'll take down the information. Just in case."

Abba gave them the address of the building.

"Apartment 3C," I said.

A few minutes later the officers had taken down all the information they needed. Four of them left in two cars. Officer Kent said he and his partner would be stationed there for the rest of their shift.

I was relieved at that.

"Come inside," Rabbi Alisha said to Abba and me. She sounded tired and sad.

As soon as we stepped through the door, I understood why.

It wasn't just the doors that had been vandalized but the entire building. Red swastikas were painted on almost every wall. Sacred prayer books had been torn apart. The pages were scattered all over. Paintings had been torn off the walls and spray-painted.

Everything was ruined.

I almost couldn't breathe. I looked at Abba. Tears were rolling down his face too.

"Who would do this?" I asked. "Who hates us this much? Who hates *anyone* this much?"

Abba put his arm around me and squeezed me tight. "I should take you home," he said.

"No." If Rabbi Alisha had to be there, I did too. "I want to stay."

Rabbi Alisha led us to the temple office. She unlocked the door and we went inside.

"At least they didn't get in here," Abba said.

"At this point, I don't think it matters," Rabbi Alisha sighed. We followed her into her inner office, where we all sat. Her big office chair had a rip in the fabric, and it squeaked when she sat down.

"What do you mean?" I asked. "How can it not matter?"

She reached for a tissue from the box on her desk and took a deep breath. "We were already on the verge of having to shut down. Even with insurance, we can't do all the repairs and replace all those books and the Torah scrolls. Some of them were basically priceless. We will have to cancel the party and refund all the tickets—and that's what was supposed to save us. Or at least buy us some time."

"There must be something we can do," Abba said.

Rabbi Alisha nudged the box of tissues toward us. Abba took four and handed me two.

"I don't think so," the rabbi said. "I feel like this was a sign. We've barely been hanging on, but then..." She gave me a half smile. "I'm so sorry, Elsie. Your idea was a great one. It might even have worked. You don't deserve to see it end like this."

I couldn't understand why anyone would want to destroy our temple. But I was more than confused—I felt heartbroken. And afraid. And really helpless.

"I should call the insurance company," Rabbi Alisha said, standing up suddenly. "I'll see you out."

She was trying to get rid of us. Maybe she wanted to be alone to cry some more. I got that.

"What about the baskets?" I asked. "Did they ruin them too?"

"Oh," Rabbi Alisha said, her eyebrows going up in surprise. "I don't know. We should go look."

Although all the decorations for the party had been ruined—every balloon popped, every streamer ripped and torn down, all the tables and chairs pushed over and more hateful symbols and words spray-painted on the walls—the vandals had left the kitchen mostly alone. Some pots and pans had been tossed around, but everything in the fridge was fine.

"Let's take the baskets as we'd planned," Abba said. "That's something we can do."

"I'm not really in the mood to spread joy," I said.

"Me either," Abba admitted. "But we carry on as planned. If they prevent us from doing our good deeds, they win, don't they?"

"I guess so," I said. Mostly because he seemed so determined.

Rabbi Alisha helped us load up the car, and then we were on our way.

Chapter Fifteen

We took some baskets to seniors in my grandparents' building that Abba knew. Thankfully,
none of them were on the third floor.

Then we took one to Bubby and Zaida. They
made tea, and we sat at the table to tell them the
bad news about the temple.

They were very sad about what had happened.

Abba also asked them about the man on the third floor.

"Mr. Berns," Bubby said. "He's a sad, lonely man who can sometimes say horrible things. It wouldn't have been him—he's basically housebound. And while he's vocal, I can't imagine he'd do something so overtly hateful."

"Or illegal," Zaida said.

Bubby looked at me. "Why didn't you tell us when it happened?"

I shrugged. "I don't know. He was mean to Grace too. I guess we just wanted to forget about it. We didn't like thinking about how mean people can be."

"I understand," Bubby said. "No one likes to think about it. It's an unfortunate reality that people like that exist. A reality we wish you never had to face. You, Grace or anyone. But some people have hate in their hearts. Sometimes they take it out on people they don't even know."

"That's not right," I said.

"No, it's not," Zaida said. "Hating someone because they're Jewish, or because of how they look, the color of their skin, their disability or" — he smiled at Abba—"who they love, is absolutely not right. No one should be hated simply because of who they are."

"Well, I hate those haters!" I said, feeling anger bubble up in me. I started to cry, but they were mad tears. I wanted to bang on the table and yell. "I hate that they destroyed our temple. I hate that they ruined our party. I hate that they ruined everything!"

"Elsie," Bubby said calmly, "I know you're upset. But that is enough."

I swallowed and took a deep breath, pressing my lips together to keep the rest of my angry words in.

Bubby went on, "There's enough hate going around. You have every right to be upset, but don't allow that to put hate into *your* heart. Hate has never solved any problems. In fact, it often creates more."

I wasn't sure what she meant, but Abba was nodding, so she was probably right. "I guess," I said.

Not long after, we left Bubby and Zaida's apartment and took the rest of the baskets to the women's shelter. They were so thankful and happy to receive them that it made us feel a little better.

Then Abba took me home. He pulled up to the front door of our building. "You going to be okay?" he asked.

I shrugged. "I guess."

"I'm still taking tonight off," he said. "The three of us will do something special. Maybe we'll go see a movie or something. Take our minds off it."

I shrugged again. "Okay."

I started to get out of the car.

"Elsie? You're my favorite. You know that, right?"

I nodded. Then, even with the armrest in the way, I leaned over to give him a hug. "You're my favorite too. I love you almost as much as I love Dad."

He laughed and squeezed me tighter before letting me go. "All right. I should get to work. Call me or Dad if you need anything, okay?"

"I will," I promised.

I had been right when I predicted I wouldn't get any homework done that afternoon.

Not because I was excited about the party but because I was heartbroken. I was also restless. I needed to do something.

What would Queen Esther do? I wondered.

She wouldn't sit at home pretending to do homework. That much I knew.

I left a note for Dad on the kitchen table, telling him where I was going. Then I bundled up in my coat and boots, grabbed my keys and left the apartment.

Chapter Sixteen

When I got to the temple, the police car was still in the parking lot. I walked up to the driver's side and waved. Officer Kent put down his window.

"Hi," I said. "Can I go inside to talk to Rabbi Alisha?"

He nodded. "Go ahead. I'm really sorry about what happened here."

I thanked him and started toward the doors. I tried not to notice the giant red symbols of hate, but it was impossible. I stood there staring. Getting angrier and angrier.

I remembered what my grandmother had said. *Hate has never solved any problems.*

I took deep breaths and was about to go in when I heard a car pull up. I turned, scared for a minute until I remembered the police were watching.

A woman got out of the car a moment later. She was Black with long, curly hair. "Are you Elsie?" she called out as she walked toward me.

"Yes?"

She gave me a big smile. "Great to meet you. I'm Ally Jackson, Grace's aunt. I'm here to do the story on the Purim party for tonight's news."

"Oh," I said. "Um, the party is canceled."

She glanced at the police car and then at the front doors. Her eyes widened when she saw the swastikas. "Oh my goodness."

"The inside is worse," I said.

"Oh no. That's terrible. I'm so sorry."

I shrugged. Everyone seemed to be sorry. But that didn't change anything.

Nothing would change if no one did anything. Queen Esther wouldn't have sat around and waited for things to change. If she had, all her people would have been killed.

"The temple is probably going to have to close," I said. "Tonight's fundraiser was our last chance to get the money to fix all the problems. But now…" I waved toward the building. "Everything's ruined."

She put her hand on my shoulder. "I'm so sorry," she repeated.

It kind of made me mad. Not at her, but still really mad. I didn't want to be helpless.

"No," I said suddenly.

"Pardon?"

"I mean, no, I'm not going to accept that the temple is doomed. Maybe we can't have the party, but we can clean up. We won't let hate get into our hearts."

I turned back toward the temple doors.

"Wait," Ally said.

I stopped and looked at her over my shoulder.

"I still want to do the story."

"I told you, the party's canceled."

"Not on the party," she said. "On *you*. And the temple. About what happened. The community should know."

"Okay, well, we should probably ask Rabbi Alisha if that's okay. We can go inside."

"Let me get my equipment."

As she rushed back to her car, I told the police officers what was happening. "Good idea," Officer Kent said. "We'll be here for another hour, and then there will be another team to replace us. We want you to feel safe. We'll find the people who did this."

"Thank you," I said.

Ally returned. She had a bag over her shoulder and was holding a big camera. "Let's go inside."

An hour later we were in the lobby, ready to start taping.

I'd explained to Rabbi Alisha (who had been on the phone all day) how I was not going to accept defeat. How I was going to channel my Queen Esther.

She still looked unsure, but she agreed to the story. We gathered around, Rabbi Alisha, Ari the admin assistant who worked in the office, Jeff the caretaker and me.

Dad had also just arrived, because the rabbi said I couldn't be on TV without a parent present.

Ally had gone outside to interview the police officers. Then she'd taken some photos of the symbols, the damaged building and the ruined social hall. Now she had her camera set up on a tripod to do the interviews.

"All right," she said. "I'm going to do a lead-in, and then I'll ask you some questions. Just act natural. Like we're having a conversation."

She took a deep breath, in and out. Then she counted down and spoke right to the camera in an announcer voice.

"Good afternoon. I'm Ally Jackson, coming to you from Temple Beth El. I was supposed to be here doing a story on a fundraiser for the synagogue, but instead I'm sorry to be reporting on the terrible hate crimes that happened here overnight. I'm here with Rabbi Alisha Wolfe. She arrived at the building this morning to find the temple had been broken into and vandalized. Rabbi, can you please tell us how you felt when you arrived this morning?"

Ally held out the microphone to Rabbi Alisha, who began to tell the story I already knew. About what had happened, how everything was destroyed.

But then she started to speak about hate crimes and antisemitism. How what the people had done wasn't just done to the building but to our people. How their trying to spread fear and hate didn't just hurt the Jewish community but *all* communities. Because if one part of the community wasn't safe, no one was safe.

It reminded me of one of her Saturday speeches. As she spoke, I reached for Dad's hand. He squeezed mine back. We watched, listening to the rabbi's words that were strong and powerful. She was channeling her Queen Esther.

I felt myself stand taller. I channeled *my* Queen Esther. I didn't want to be afraid. I didn't want to give up. I wanted to be strong and fierce and do whatever needed to be done to save the temple. Starting that very moment.

As Rabbi Alisha continued to speak, I let Dad's hand go and started picking up prayer books, stacking them on a cart. I made two piles, one for ruined books and one for books that weren't damaged. The ruined pile got higher and higher.

"And here we have Elsie, one of the young temple members, who I know was looking forward to the party tonight."

I looked up, and there was Ally with her microphone pointed at me. "Hi," I said. But I didn't stop picking up books. Dad whispered my name, but I kept on gathering books.

"You look very determined, Elsie," Ally said.

I nodded. "We need to clean up. We don't have any money, and tonight's fundraiser was supposed to save the temple. I don't know how we'll save it now, but I'm not going to let hate get into my heart.

Like Queen Esther, I'm going to be strong and brave."

I noticed movement out of the corner of my eye. It was Dad, wiping a tear away with his thumb. But he was smiling and nodding at me.

"I think you already are strong and brave," Ally said. Then she looked at the camera. "We're going to stay on top of this story at Temple Beth El. I'll be following up with the police to find out if they have any leads on who might be behind this hate crime. Until then, if you'd like to make any donations to assist the temple, we'll have the information on our website. This is Ally Jackson reporting live. Back to you at the desk, Sandra."

She stared at the camera for a few more seconds, then exhaled loudly. "And we're out," she said in her regular voice as she clicked off the camera.

"Thank you," Rabbi Alisha said.

"Now," Ally said. She looked around and pushed up her sleeves. "How can I help?"

An hour after that Grace arrived with her family, ready to pitch in.

Then Abba showed up with the entire cast of *Fiddler on the Roof* and everyone else from the theater. They had canceled the evening's production so they could come help out. Bella gave me a giant hug and kiss on the cheek before she grabbed a garbage bag and got to work.

The funeral director came to take away the damaged prayer books. We learned you couldn't throw them out, even single pages that had been torn from the books. Because they were sacred, they had to be buried respectfully at the cemetery.

Then a group of off-duty police officers and other first responders arrived with more cleaning supplies and cans of paint.

The caterers showed up with vans full of food. They said they had it ready for the party anyway and might as well feed the huge crowd of people helping. They set up their buffet right there in the lobby and started feeding all the helpers.

That's when Rabbi Alisha burst into tears. When I tried to comfort her, she assured me they were happy tears.

The helpers just kept coming. A group from a mosque down the road, Dad's work friends, a couple of women from the shelter we'd taken baskets to. Even my grandparents and tons of other seniors from their building.

At one point Rabbi Alisha got on the sound system and announced it was time for a break and for everyone to grab a seat.

She stood at the front of the crowd and waited for everyone to settle.

"I'm a little overwhelmed, honestly," she said. "But I want to thank everyone for coming out to help.

I…it means a lot. I'm going to start crying soon, so I'll leave it at that, but I do want you all to know how much I—and the rest of the Temple Beth El family—appreciate your being here."

The crowd all clapped.

"And while I don't want to take much more of your time that you have so generously already given us, it *is* Purim, and that means it is our custom to read the Book of Esther. We would have read it at our party, but, well, I guess *this* is our party now. Welcome! The food is good but,"—she made a face—"the decor could use some work."

Everyone laughed.

"I understand if you don't want to stay for our reading," the rabbi said. "No hard feelings if you want to leave now."

Not one person moved. The rabbi's smile widened, even though she looked like she was really going to start crying.

"Wonderful." She cleared her throat. "I will read it in English so everyone can understand. But I will need audience participation. When we hear the name Haman, it is customary to make noise to show displeasure. We try to block out his name because he is the evil villain of the story. Normally we would use noisemakers—what we call graggers—but using our voices and stomping our feet will work as well."

Abba stood up. "Wait!" he yelled.

Everyone turned.

"We have talented performers here." He pointed toward where all the theater people sat. "Maybe they wouldn't mind improvising the story while you read it, Rabbi."

Rabbi Alisha laughed. "That sounds perfect, if they wouldn't mind lending their skills."

All the actors who had come from the theater with Abba stood up and came to the front of the hall. Even without costumes, they took on their roles perfectly. Everyone in the building was rapt as they watched the story play out, many for the first time. The room was silent but for the rabbi's reading. Until Haman was mentioned, of course. Then everyone yelled and screamed and stomped their feet, blotting out the name of the man who wanted to kill Queen Esther's people. My people.

I looked around at everyone—Abba, Dad, Grace and her family, friends, temple members and strangers. Even though we yelled and screamed Haman's name, we were celebrating. Because even though someone had tried to hate us and scare us, we had come together and persevered. Just like Queen Esther and her people.

And maybe the most important thing? We hadn't let the hate into our hearts.

It was the best reading of the book of Esther there had ever been. At least in my opinion.

After the reading and all the applause, we got back to work.

It wasn't the night I'd planned, but it was the best night of my life.

Which was weird. I didn't win the contest, because there wasn't one. I didn't get to show off my costume. There wasn't even any dancing. But I felt part of something bigger than just a party. I felt part of a community.

A few hours later, when we were all dusty and tired, Rabbi Alisha came on the sound system again to announce that we were done for the night. She thanked us for working so hard.

Then, just as people started toward the door, voices began to sing. Beautiful voices. Everyone stopped in their tracks and turned back to see the actors on the stage. They were standing together arm in arm, singing.

I knew that song. I looked up at Abba and Dad. They knew it too. Their smiles were wide, and they had tears in their eyes.

It was one of my favorite songs—"To Life" from

Fiddler on the Roof. It was about how we should be joyful no matter what. To celebrate and be happy with what we have. As I looked around, I realized I had a lot. I also knew, with my whole heart, that somehow we would save the temple.

Abba put his arm around me. Dad put his hand on my shoulder. I couldn't imagine anywhere I'd rather be.

We began to sing along, raising our voices with so many others, singing with joy in our hearts.

It was the perfect end to a not-so-perfect day.

Acknowledgments

The list of people to thank for helping put together the fine piece of literature you hold in your hands is shorter than for most of my books. But that doesn't mean I appreciate each of them any less. My books always take a village—some large and some small—and I wouldn't have it any other way.

Thank you to the Jewish Kidlit Mavens for inspiring me to write another book about contemporary Jewish kids and reassuring me that I was on the right track. A giant thank-you to Heidi Rabinowitz and Susan Kusel for heading up this great group. Do you two ever sleep?

To Chris Tebbetts and Susan Kusel (again!) who read early versions of this book, thank you both for helping me fix the details I didn't know that I didn't know.

A big thanks, as always, to Andrew Wooldridge for his commitment to publishing diverse and exceptional books by Canadian creators. Your hard work and dedication are always appreciated.

Thank you to Ella Collier for creating the perfect cover and making Elsie so real in my head.

To the rest of the Orca pod: Ruth, Olivia, Margaret, Kennedy, Susan, Leslie, Vivian and everyone else who had a hand in this project— thank you again for enabling me to put my name on another book I'm so very proud of.

And thanks to my editor, Tanya Trafford, the person I dedicated this book to, because she is fierce and smart and I would totally want her as the Wonder Woman to my Queen Esther. Hamantaschen for everyone!

Thank you to Hilary McMahon for the chats and career advice and for generally being awesome on top of all that contract stuff.

Thank you to Deke, husband, plot assistor, top fan, purse-holder, book-flapper, chauffeur and all-around excellent partner.

No thanks to the cat who barfed during the writing of these acknowledgments. Nor to the other one who I had to yell at (again) to stop licking the dog.

BUBBY ROSE'S FAMOUS HAMANTASCHEN

These triangular cookies made during the Jewish festival of Purim are named for Haman, the villain found in the Book of Esther.

They were traditionally filled with a prune or poppyseed paste, but apricot jam or your favorite chocolate spread would also be delicious. Anything goes! (Okay, maybe not olive paste or relish.)

Makes about 24 cookies.

INGREDIENTS:

1/2 cup butter, at room temperature (you can use margarine if you want to keep the recipe pareve)

6 tablespoons sugar

1 egg

1 teaspoon vanilla

1 1/2 cups flour

Filling of choice (about **1/2 cup**)

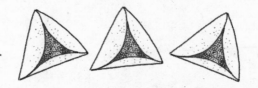

FOR THE DOUGH:

1. With a wooden spoon, beat butter and sugar until light and creamy.
2. Add egg and vanilla and beat for two more minutes. Sift in flour and mix until well combined.

FOR THE COOKIES:

1. Preheat oven to 350°F. Grease two baking sheets or line with parchment paper.
2. Roll out dough on a floured surface to 1/4-inch thickness. Using a round cookie cutter or large glass, cut out circles in the dough.
3. Place the circles on the baking sheets and spoon one teaspoon of filling into the center of each circle. Don't overfill!
4. For each circle, turn up one side and pinch the corner closed. Do this two more times to make a triangular "pocket" around the filling. The cookie should now look a bit like a pirate hat.
5. Bake for 15 minutes or so, until edges are golden. Remove from the oven and cool.
6. Hand them out and impress all your friends!

Joanne Levy is the author of a number of books for young people, including *Double Trouble* and *Fish Out of Water* in the Orca Currents line and the middle-grade novels *Sorry for Your Loss*, *The Sun Will Come Out* and *Small Medium At Large*, which was nominated for the Red Maple Award. Joanne lives in Clinton, Ontario.

For more information on all the books

in the Orca Currents line, please visit

orcabook.com